Katy

THE FOLLETT BEGINNING-TO-READ SERIES

One Day
Everything
Went Wrong

ELIZABETH VREEKEN

Illustrated by Leonard Shortall

Cover painting by Mary Stevens

Follett Publishing Company

CHICAGO

Library of Congress Catalog Card Number: 66-13711

ISBN 0-695-46550-3 Library edition
ISBN 0-695-36550-9 Paper edition

Ninth Printing

Billy was seven years old.

He liked to do lots of things.

He liked to play with his dog.

He liked to watch television
and to read books.

But most of all, he liked to help.

He helped his father and his mother.

He helped his teacher and his neighbors.

He was always looking for somebody
to help.

Everybody said, "What a fine helping
boy Billy is!"

But one day, everything went wrong.

It was Saturday.

There was no school.

Billy had lots of time to play.

Billy had lots of time to help.

He went into the kitchen.

Mother was baking a cake.

"May I help you, Mother?" asked Billy.

"Not now, dear," said Mother.

"The cake is almost done.

I am whipping the cream for it."

Just then the telephone rang.

Mother went to answer it.

"I know," said Billy.

"I will finish whipping the cream."

He whipped and he whipped.

The cream got thicker and thicker.

It began to turn yellow.

Soon Mother came back.

"Oh, Billy," she cried.

"You have whipped the cream too long.

It has turned to butter!"

"I am sorry, Mother," said Billy.

"I just wanted to help."

"I know," said Mother.

"Never mind. I will make a
chocolate icing instead.

But, please, Billy, go and
help somebody else!"

Billy sat and thought.

"I know," he said.

"I will give Tippy a bath.
I will surprise Daddy."

He went into the bathroom.

He put water into the tub.

He put in some of Mother's
bubble bath, too.

Then he went to find Tippy.

Tippy had never liked water
very much.

He did not like it at all with bubbles.

He jumped from the tub.

He was covered with soapsuds.

He ran down the stairs and into
the street.

"Mad dog! Mad dog!"
called all the people.

They ran into their houses.

Somebody called a policeman.

When Tippy saw Policeman Bird,
he stopped running.

Tippy knew Policeman Bird.

He went to him wagging his tail.

Soon Billy got there.

"What happened to Tippy, Billy?"
asked Policeman Bird.

"I was giving him a bath," said Billy.

"Daddy doesn't like to do it.
I just wanted to help."

"Well," said Policeman Bird.

"Take Tippy home and wash him off.
And, please, Billy, go and help
somebody else!"

Billy did as he was told.

Then he sat on the porch and thought.

"I know," he said.

"I will help Mr. Dean next door.

He did not finish weeding his garden last night.

I will do it for him."

Soon he was busy in Mr. Dean's garden.

When Mr. Dean got home,
he began to shout.

"Who was in my garden?

Who pulled out all the flowers
I planted?"

Poor Billy!

He wanted to run and hide.

But he didn't.

"I did it, Mr. Dean," he said.

"I thought they were weeds.

I am sorry. I just wanted to help."

"I know that you did not
mean it, Billy," said Mr. Dean.

"I am sorry I was so angry.

But, please, Billy, go and help
somebody else!"

Poor Billy!

Everything was going wrong.

And he just wanted to help.

"I know," he said.

"I will go to see Grandma.

Maybe I can help her."

Billy walked down the street

to his Grandma's house.

"Grandma, I have been trying
to help people all day.

But everything is going wrong."

"Well, I was just going to clean
Joey's cage, Billy," said Grandma.

"Why don't you try helping me
with that."

Joey was Grandma's little parakeet.

Billy loved him.

Joey knew Billy and loved him too.

First Billy took out the tray
at the bottom of the cage.

He cleaned it so that it shone.

"There, you did that just fine, Billy,"
said Grandma.

Billy was happy.

He thought his bad day was over.

He said to Joey,

"Would you like a bath now?"

He filled Joey's little bathtub
with nice cool water.

He lifted the cage just a little
to move the tub under.

In a flash Joey was out of the cage.

He flew all around the room.

Then he saw an open window.

He flew out.

Grandma was sad.

"Oh, my dear little Joey!

I'll never get him back," she said.

"Don't worry, Grandma," said Billy.
"Everything is going wrong today.
But I will make it all right this time.
I will get Joey back for you.
I have a plan."

First Billy put the clean tray
back in the cage.

Then he took the cage
out to the porch.

He sat on the steps beside the cage.

He began to call to Joey.

He said all the things Joey could say.

He said,

"Come on! Come over here!

Give me a kiss!"

He said, "He's a good boy!

Such a good boy!"

He said these things over
and over again.

He rang the little bell
in Joey's cage.

Soon Joey flew out of the tree.

He sat on the fence.

He looked at Billy.

Billy kept talking to him.

Soon Joey answered,
"He's a good boy!
Such a good boy!"
Billy held out his finger.
He called,
"Come on, Joey!
Come over here!
Give me a kiss!"

Joey flew a little closer.

"He's a good boy!

Such a good boy!" he called.

Suddenly he flew to Billy's finger.

Very slowly Billy put him into his cage.

Joey went right to his seed cup.

What a hungry bird he was!

Billy closed the cage door.

Then he called, "Come, Grandma!
Your Joey is back!"

Grandma was so happy!

She hugged Billy over and over.

But soon Billy was on his way again.

Maybe he was looking for somebody
to help.

ONE DAY EVERYTHING WENT WRONG

One Day Everything Went Wrong has a total vocabulary of 264 words. Regular possessives and contractions (-'s, -n't, -'ll, -'m) and regular verb forms (-s, -ed, -ing) of words already on the list are not listed separately, but the endings are given in parentheses after the words.

5 Billy ('s)	but	everything	done
was	most	went	am
seven	all	wrong	whipping (ed)
years	help (ed) (ing)	there	cream
old	**6** father	no	it
he ('s)	mother ('s)	school	just
like (d)	teacher	had	then
to	neighbors	time	telephone
do	always	into	rang
lots	looking (ed)	the	answer (ed)
of	for	kitchen	know
things	somebody	baking	will
play	everybody	cake	finish
with	said	may	got
his	what	I ('ll)	thicker
dog	a	you	began
watch	fine	asked	turn (ed)
television	boy	**8** not	yellow
and	is	now	soon
read	**7** one	dear	came
books	day	almost	back

oh
she
cried
have
too
long
has
butter
10 sorry
wanted
never
mind
make
chocolate
icing
instead
please
go (ing)
else
11 sat
thought
give
Tippy
bath
surprise
Daddy
bathroom
put
water
tub
in
some
bubble (s)
find
12 had
very
much
did (n't)
at
all
jumped
from
covered
soapsuds
ran
down

stairs
street
13 mad
call (ed)
people
they
their
house (s)
policeman
when
saw
Bird
stopped
running
knew
him
wagging
tail
14 happened
doesn't
well
take
home
wash
off
15 as
was
told
on
porch
Mr. Dean ('s)
next
door
weeding
garden
last
night
busy
16 shout
who
my
pulled
out
flowers
planted
poor

run
hide
were
weeds
that
mean
so
angry
18 see
Grandma ('s)
maybe
can
her
walked
19 been
try (ing)
day
clean (ed)
Joey ('s)
cage
why
me
20 little
parakeet
loved
first
took
tray
bottom
shone
21 happy
bad
over
would
filled
bathtub
nice
cool
lifted
move
under
22 flash
flew
around
room
an

open
window
sad
get
23 worry
today
right
this
have
plan
24 steps
beside
could
say
come
here
give
kiss
good
such
26 these
again
rang
bell
tree
fence
kept
talking
27 held
finger
28 closer
suddenly
slowly
seed
cup
hungry
29 closed
your
hugged
way
where

Humorously told familiar stories are a unique part of the Follett Beginning-To-Read Series. Each book uses easy vocabulary to tell a complete story in a funny, appealing style. With Follett Beginning-To-Read books, children can enjoy reading real books on their own early in their reading experience. All books in this series are colorfully illustrated.

Follett Beginning-To-Read books that you will enjoy:

The Dog Who Came to Dinner
By Sydney Taylor

Know When to Stop
By Valjean McLenighan

The Little Red Hen
By Jean Horton Berg

Mabel the Whale
By Patricia King

The No-Bark Dog
By Stan Williamson

What You See Is What You Get
By Valjean McLenighan